AF575504

SNEAK PEEK
@ SNEAKERS
NIKE
Kerrily Sapet

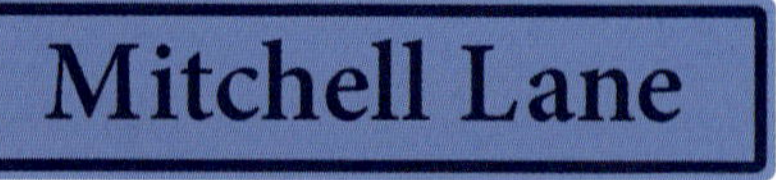

PUBLISHERS

mitchelllane.com

2001 SW 31st Avenue
Hallandale, FL 33009

First Edition, 2021.
Author: Kerrily Sapet
Designer: Ed Morgan
Editor: Sharon F. Doorasamy

Series: Sneak Peek @ Sneakers
Title: Nike / by Kerrily Sapet

Hallandale, FL : Mitchell Lane Publishers, [2021]

Library bound ISBN: 978-1-68020-648-7
eBook ISBN: 978-1-68020-649-4

PHOTO CREDITS: cover: shutterstock, p. 5 SUE OGROCKI/REUTERS/Newscom, p. 6 STEVE MARCUS/REUTERS/Newscom, p. 8 shutterstock, p. 11 freepik.com, pp. 12-13 Jon Tyson on Unsplash, p. 17 shutterstock, p. 19 BRENDAN MCDERMID/REUTERS/Newscom, p. 21 shutterstock, pp. 22-23 shutterstock, p. 24 freepik.com, p. 25 nasa.gov, p. 27 JD1/WENN/Newscom, p. 29 José Cruz/ABr CC-BY-SA-3.0

CONTENTS

chapter 1

AIR JORDAN

The seconds ticked away as Michael Jordan dribbled down the basketball court. He was exhausted. His team was losing the NBA Championship game. With six seconds left in the game, Jordan saw his chance. He jumped and let the basketball fly. It arced over the other players, spun toward the basket, and swished through the net. The Chicago Bulls won the championship title!

Change to “Michael Jordan is a real-life super hero,” said Phil Jackson, coach of the Chicago Bulls. In his career, Jordan won six NBA championships. He also won two Olympic gold medals. He was known for taking long flying leaps and slam-dunking the ball. Fans called him “His Airness,” “Air Jordan,” and “GOAT.” GOAT stands for the “Greatest of All Time.” Even Michael Jordan’s shoes were famous.

The inspiration for Michael Jordan’s trademark “tongue-out” habit came from watching his dad, who had the same quirk when working on cars or fixing things around the house.

chapter 1

When Jordan started playing in the NBA, Nike designed bright red and black basketball shoes for his size 13 feet. People called them "the devil's shoes." The NBA said they were illegal. They weren't white like other basketball shoes. They fined him $5,000.00 every time he wore them in a game. Jordan wore the shoes anyway. They became a symbol of rebellion, power, and success. Kids wanted to wear them too. In 1985, Nike released a red and black sneaker called the Air Jordan 1. Its **logo** pictured Jordan jumping through the air with the ball. Fans bought 1 million pairs in a single month.

NBA basketball legend Michael Jordan wore this signed pair of Nike Air Jordan 1 in his rookie season.

Many years before athletes started wearing high-tech, flashy sneakers, shoes were simple. They protected people's feet from hot sand, snow, rocks, and sticks. And they weren't always comfortable. Right and left shoes were the same shape. People stuffed grass in the bottom for cushioning. Some of the first athletic shoes were made from rubber and a thick fabric called canvas. In winter, the rubber soles froze and cracked. In summer, they melted into sticky globs. In 1839, American inventor Charles Goodyear created a stronger, more flexible rubber by mixing rubber with different chemicals. Goodyear named it **vulcanized rubber**, after Vulcan, the Roman god of fire.

Rubber-soled shoes soon became popular. They were called "sneakers" because the soles were so quiet. People could sneak up on each other. Today, more people wear sneakers than any other type of shoe. Nike sells 25 pairs every second!

FAST FACT:

The world's oldest running shoe—made 160 years ago—is a stiff leather dress shoe with two thick metal spikes hammered into the toe and heel.

TENNIES, TRAINERS, AND TAKKIES

People around the world call sneakers by different names. In the eastern United States, they're "sneakers." In the Midwest, they're "tennis shoes." Sneakers are also known as "gym shoes," "kicks," "daps," "gutties," and "plimsolls" because early rubber-soled shoes had a stripe like a line called a "plimsoll" on a boat. Whatever the name, they're the most popular shoes on Earth.

chapter 2

RUBBER WAFFLES

Bill Bowerman was a track coach at the University of Oregon in the 1960s. He was known for being "a thinker and a tinkerer." He spent hours in his garage making lightweight running shoes. Bowerman sawed shoes apart and studied them. He experimented with new materials, such as kangaroo leather, velvet, rattlesnake, and fish skin. "A shoe must be three things," Bowerman said. "It must be light, comfortable, and it's got to go the distance."

Phil Knight was a runner on the team. He tested a pair of Bowerman's shoes. The shoes were made with white rubbery fabric. When Knight took a business class, he thought about Bowerman's **innovative** shoes and got an idea. He would buy high quality, inexpensive, running shoes made by Onitsuka Tiger, a Japanese company. Then he'd sell them to Americans. Onitsuka Tiger made three designs. They were the "Limber Up" for training, the "Spring Up" for jumping, and the "Throw Up" for throwing a discus.

chapter 2

This marble sculpture of the goddess Nike, also known as the Nike of Samothrace, is prominently displayed in the Louvre Museum in Paris, France. It is one of the most celebrated sculptures in the world.

In 1964, Knight and Bowerman teamed up. Each contributed $500.00 to start a company called Blue Ribbon Sports. They initially bought 300 pairs of "Limber Ups." Knight and Bowerman ending up selling 1,300 pairs the first year. Knight's mother bought one of the first pairs. Runners loved the shoes. The business grew fast. Soon Knight and Bowerman decided to start a new company, using Bowerman's designs. They opened an office in Beaverton, Oregon. Their salesman, Jeff Johnson, suggested "Nike." Nike is the name of the Greek goddess of victory. Nobody liked it. At first, people thought the lettering said, "Mike." They soon learned it was "Nike," and it rhymed with "spiky."

chapter 2

Coach Bowerman continued inventing new designs. One morning at breakfast, he looked at a plate of waffles. He realized a shoe with waffle-like soles could grip the ground better. Bowerman poured melted rubber into the waffle iron. The rubber glued the waffle iron shut. But he kept trying. Soon, Bowerman had developed a new sole. When U.S. runners wore them at the 1972 Olympic trials, people called them "moon shoes." That's because their footprints looked like the ones left by astronauts on the moon. Bowerman improved on the design. Nike started selling a shoe called the Waffle Trainer.

Runners liked the fit and feel of Bowerman's designs. More and more people began to buy Nikes. Today, Nike has offices in 45 countries. **Consumers** worldwide spend $50 million a day on Nike sneakers.

SWOOSH

When Phil Knight asked Carolyn Davidson, a college student, to design Nike's logo she drew chunky lightning bolts, thick squiggles, and a curvy check mark. Knight picked the check mark because it resembled the goddess Nike's wing. He called it the "Swoosh," like the sound of running fast. Davidson charged $35.00 to design one of the world's most famous logos.

chapter 3

SNEAKERS EVERYWHERE

Early on, sneakers were only worn by athletes. In the 1950s, a sneaker craze swept the country. Sneakers were more comfortable and less expensive than leather shoes. People, especially kids, wanted to wear the same sneakers as athletes and movie stars. Today everyone wears sneakers, from babies taking their first steps to grandfathers pushing walkers.

Sneakers are made in all sizes, shapes, and styles. There are high-tops, low-tops, slip-ons, sneaker boots, and even high-heeled sneakers. They come in a rainbow of colors, from plain white to sparkly dragon green with neon purple stripes. Sneakers tie, zip, snap, Velcro, and button.

By the 1980s, Nike was making shoes for running, basketball, tennis, soccer, golf, football, skateboarding, and even cycling. They sold shoes to everyone from Olympic athletes to dog walkers. "If you have a body, you're an athlete," said Bill Bowerman.

Nike competes with other companies to release new shoe designs every year. Companies **sponsor** athletes. They pay them to wear and advertise their sneakers and sportswear. Nike sponsors college and pro teams, Olympic teams, and athletes, such as Tiger Woods, LeBron James, Serena Williams, and Cristiano Ronaldo. In 1995, Sheryl Swoopes became the first woman athlete to get a signature Nike basketball shoe with the release of the Air Swoopes. Sneaker companies also work with pop stars and artists to design shoes. Nike has partnered with Kanye West, Travis Scott, and even television networks to create themed shoes.

Nike manufactures its shoes in countries such as Vietnam, Korea, and India. New robotic assembly lines can crank out 1 million sneakers a year. From the factories, shoes are loaded onto ships, planes, and trains and sent to nearly every country in the world. Experts predict by 2025, people will spend $95 billion a year on sneakers.

FAST FACT:

Customers who visit Niketowns, Nike's biggest stores, can test their shoes on mini basketball courts and soccer fields. They can also choose custom colors for their shoes. In 2019, Nike earned $39 billion selling sneakers and sportswear.

chapter 4

SNEAKER TECH

Designing a new sneaker can take months. The process starts with the **designer** thinking about the purpose of the shoe and the needs of the person wearing it. Baseball players want shoes with cleats that grip soft grass and dirt. Runners like lightweight shoes with cushioning and reflective materials for running at night. Individuals with disabilities might need a shoe that's easy to slip on and off, like the one Nike designed with a strap and zipper at the heel.

Designers start by making sketches. They think about weight, comfort, and materials. Most shoes are made from rubber, leather, plastic, fabric, and **synthetics**. Synthetics are combinations of man-made materials. To add cushioning, designers use gels, foams, and even trapped air bubbles, an idea Frank Rudy, a NASA engineer, pitched to Nike.

Designers often get their ideas from the world around them. A World War II fighter plane inspired Nike designer Tinker Hatfield's design for the Air Jordan V. Hatfield designed a shoe with teeth-like flames on the side, like a plane he saw. A red and black lawnmower inspired Hatfield's design for the Air Jordan XI. Like the lawnmower, the shoes needed to survive bumps and crashes. Hatfield used thick, shiny, black leather for the sides and tough red rubber on the soles.

Designers use the latest technologies to improve sneakers. They are experimenting with 3-D printers to make **prototypes** and custom-fit shoes. New designs feature self-tying shoelaces, candy-like plastic beads that add bouncy cushioning, and sensors that can identify the person wearing the shoe.

chapter 4

Many companies are creating environmentally friendly sneakers. Nike's Trash Talk shoe is assembled from scraps of fabric and leather swept up from factory floors. Their Flyknit fabric uses recycled yarn. Companies are making shoes from fishing nets and plastic garbage removed from the ocean. Another company, Rothy's, shreds used plastic water bottles and feeds the plastic flakes into 3-D printers to create shoes.

No matter the size, shape, or color, new sneaker designs are packed with the latest technology. They are made with everything from trash to materials inspired by spiderwebs. They are designed to improve people's lives—helping them to be faster, fitter, and more comfortable.

FROM SPACESUITS TO SNEAKERS

Technology developed by NASA, the National Aeronautics and Space Administration, has changed life on Earth. NASA scientists developed a process called "blow rubber molding" to create lightweight, strong space helmets. Today, shoe companies use blow rubber molding to make sneakers with soles that can be filled with shock-absorbing materials. Millions of sneaker wearers walk in astronaut-inspired shoes every day.

chapter 5

IT'S GOTTA BE THE SHOES

People on every continent wear sneakers. They choose their sneakers for sports, for style, or to be like their favorite athlete or celebrity. Sneaker **slogans** like Nike's *Just Do It* and *Be Legendary* encourage people to be stronger and faster.

When Nike released the Air Jordan in 1985, kids wanted a pair to "Be Like Mike," as one ad said. Wearing Air Jordans was like proving they could grow up to do great things. "It's not just about the flyness of the sneaker itself," says Darryl McDaniels of the 1980s hip-hop band Run-D.M.C. "It's about the flyness positivity power and potential of the person wearing the sneakers."

Companies partner with athletes, actors, and musicians to create new designs. Rappers drop the names of shoes in songs. Celebrities post pictures of themselves on social media wearing the hottest sneaker fashions. Nike has worked with *Vogue* editor Anna Wintour, Justin Timberlake, and fashionista Aleali May, the first woman to design an Air Jordan sneaker. "People as diverse as Michael Jordan, Kurt Cobain, and Mr. Rogers are all associated with sneakers," said sneaker book author Nick Smith.

Justin Timberlake's fifth album, *Man of the Woods*, inspired the design of a special-themed Air Jordan 3 which sold out instantly after he performed in the kicks at the Super Bowl Halftime Show in 2018.

chapter 5

When sneaker companies release new shoes, people often line up to buy them. Some even camp out in rain and snow. Often companies release shoes on weekends, so school-age buyers won't skip school to get them. Internet sites crash as thousands of people try to buy the latest style. New releases often sell out in minutes. That is what happened when Nike released its Air Jordan design and SpongeBob SquarePants-themed shoes.

"Sneakerheads," a nickname for shoe collectors, sometimes spend thousands of dollars to buy a single pair of used sneakers. They love wearing sneakers, trading and selling sneakers, and adding shoes to their collections. "I had no idea it would get this big and become this important to people all over the world," says Tinker Hatfield. "Sneakers have become a part of people remembering their life."

Sneakers are more than just the rubber and fabric you wear on your feet for gym class. Today's kicks have been inspired by waffle irons and astronaut boots. Who knows what sneakers in the future will look like?

SPIKE LEE

Spike Lee is an American filmmaker who loves basketball and collecting sneakers. Many of the characters in his movies wear Nikes. Lee teamed up with Michael Jordan to make commercials selling Air Jordans. "It's Gotta be the Shoes," Lee told viewers. In 2019, Lee won an Oscar at the Academy Awards while wearing a pair of gleaming gold Air Jordans.

GLOSSARY

consumer
Someone who buys goods or services for personal use

designer
A person who creates original products

innovative
New and different

logo
A picture or symbol

prototype
The first design or model

slogan
A saying used to advertise an item

sponsor
A company that pays someone to advertise or wear their product

synthetics
Man-made materials

vulcanized rubber
Rubber mixed with chemicals to become stronger

TIMELINE

1971 Phil Knight and Bill Bowerman found Nike; Bowerman invents the Waffle Trainer.

1985 Nike releases the Air Jordan 1.

1988 Nike launches the "Just Do It" ad campaign.

1990 First Niketown store opens in Portland, Oregon.

1995 Nike released the first-ever women's signature basketball shoe, the Air Swoopes.

1996 Nike starts sponsoring Tiger Woods.

1999 Co-founder Bill Bowerman passes away.

2003 Nike signs Lebron James and Kobe Bryant.

2019 Nike earned $39 billion selling sneakers and sportswear.

FURTHER READING

Andersen, Kirsten. *Who is Michael Jordan?* New York, NY: Penguin Publishing, 2019.

Keyser, Amber J. *Sneaker Century: A History of Athletic Shoes*. Minneapolis, MN: Twenty-First Century Books, 2015.

Le Maux, Mathieu. *1000 Sneakers: A Guide to the World's Greatest Kicks, from Sport to Street*. New York, NY: Rizzoli Publications, 2016.

Nelson, Robin. *From Leather to Basketball Shoes*. Minneapolis, MN: Lerner Publishing Group, 2014.

Sichol, Lowey Bundy. *From an Idea to Nike*. New York, NY: Houghton Mifflin Harcourt Publishing Company, 2019.

INDEX

ABOUT THE AUTHOR

Kerrily Sapet has written more than 30 books for children. Sapet likes wearing black Converse low-tops. She ran her first 5K wearing a pair of blue Nikes.